A note from the author

I am thrilled that *Where's My Teddy?* has remained in print long enough to have the honour of a 25th anniversary edition. Once upon a time I was delighted when children told me it was their favourite story, now I am just as likely to hear the same from parents who grew up reading it.

Where's My Teddy? sprang out of my love of playing with words and rhymes. It's a childish pleasure and perhaps that's partly why children enjoy this story – in which Eddy's teddy is, of course, named Freddy. What else?

Behind the wordplay the book explores the subject of fear, especially in relation to being small. It's an important subject if you are four and the world around you is very big and populated by giants called grown-ups. Although Eddy is scared by the great big bear, he discovers that the bear is scared too and that he needs his teddy just as much as Eddy needs Freddy. By the end of the book Eddy's heart may be racing, but he has learned that the world is not quite such a scary place after all. I think the same goes for the bear, and maybe for the reader too.

Jez Alborough

For my dearest Rikka

First published 1992 by Walker Books Ltd
87 Vauxhall Walk, London SE11 5HJ

This edition published 2017

4 6 8 10 9 7 5 3

© 1992 Jez Alborough

The right of Jez Alborough to be identified as author/illustrator
of this work has been asserted by him in accordance
with the Copyright, Designs and Patents Act 1988

This book has been typeset in Garamond

Printed in China

British Library Cataloguing in Publication Data:
a catalogue record for this book is available from the British Library

ISBN 978-1-4063-7366-0

www.walker.co.uk
jezalborough.com

WHERE'S MY TEDDY?

JEZ ALBOROUGH

WALKER BOOKS
AND SUBSIDIARIES
LONDON · BOSTON · SYDNEY · AUCKLAND

Eddy's off to find his teddy.
Eddy's teddy's name is Freddy.

He lost him in the wood somewhere.
It's dark and horrible in there.

"Help!" said Eddy. "I'm scared already!
I want my bed! I want my teddy!"

He tip-toed
on and on
until …

something
made him stop
quite still.

A GIANT TEDDY BEAR!
"Is it Freddy?" said Eddy.
"What a surprise!
How *did* you get to be this size?"

"You're too big to huddle and cuddle," he said,

"and I'll never fit both of us into my bed."

Then out of the darkness,
clearer and clearer,
the sound of a sobbing
came nearer and nearer.

Soon the whole wood
could hear the voice bawl,
"How did you get to be
tiddly and small?
You're too small to
huddle and cuddle," it said,
"and you'll only get lost
in my giant-sized bed!"

It was a gigantic bear
and a tiddly teddy
stomping towards ...

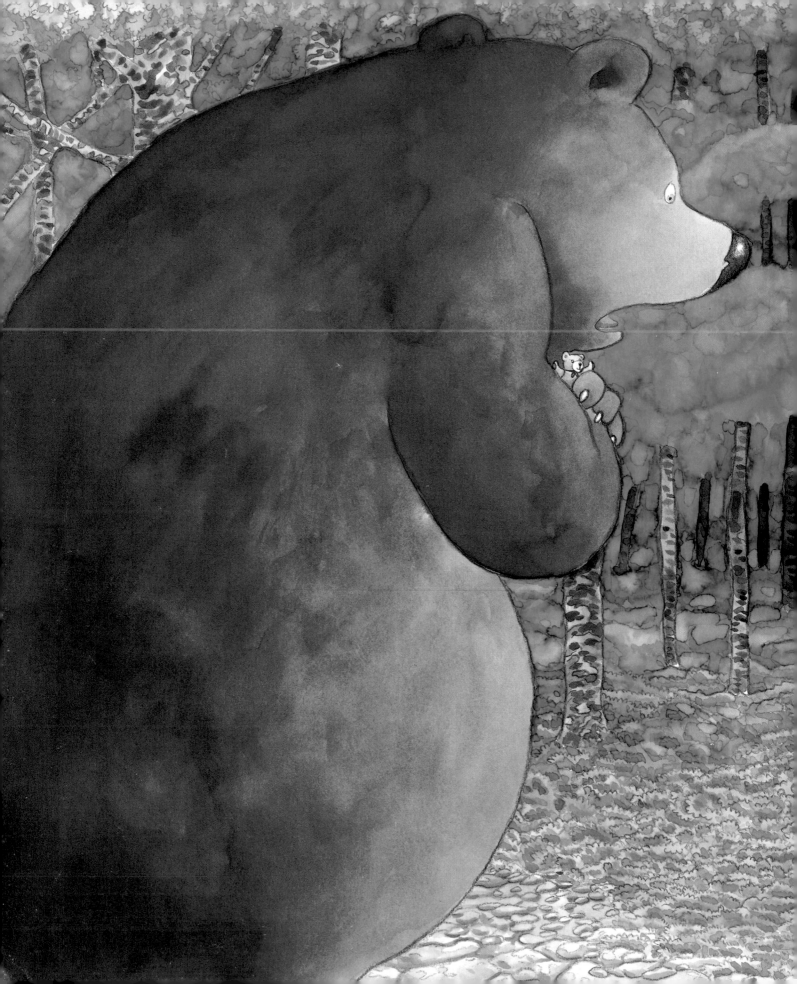

the giant teddy and Eddy.

"MY TED!"
gasped the bear.
"A BEAR!"
screamed Eddy.

"A BOY!"
yelled the bear.
"MY TEDDY!"
cried Eddy.

Then they ran and they ran
through the dark wood
back to their homes
as quick as they could ...

all the way back
to their snuggly beds,
where they huddled
and cuddled their
own little teds.

BOOKS BY JEZ ALBOROUGH

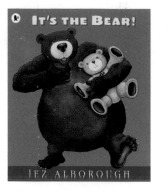

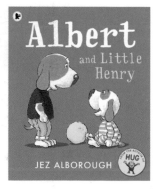

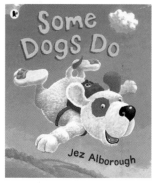

JezAlborough.com

Available from all good booksellers

www.walker.co.uk